Be Nice, Nanette!

Based on the TV series *Angela Anaconda*®
Created by Joanna Ferrone and Sue Rose as seen on the Fox Family Channel®

SIMON SPOTLIGHT
An imprint of Simon & Schuster Children's Publishing Division
1230 Avenue of the Americas, New York, New York 10020

Manufactured in the United States of America

First Edition
2 4 6 8 10 9 7 5 3 1

ISBN 0-689-83997-9

Library of Congress Control Number 00-107922

Be Nice, Nanette!

adapted by Sarah Willson

based on the scripts by
Ford Riley and Peter Elwell

illustrated by Elizabeth Brandt

Simon Spotlight

New York   London   Toronto   Sydney   Singapore

Story Number One

ice BREAKERS

CHAPTER ONE

If you'd like to know what my name is, it is Angela Anaconda of the third grade, taught by Mrs. Brinks. At my school, Tapwater Springs Elementary, I am mostly good, except for some of the time. And those times are practically always on account of a person in my class named Nanette Manoir, who pretends to be French but is not. She is the person who bugs me the most of anyone else. So you won't be surprised when I tell you about how she ruined my first-ever ice-skating lesson.

First of all, I just have to say I was really excited about learning how to ice-skate. And my dad is driving me and my friends Gina Lash and Johnny Abatti to our first-ever skating lesson any of us have ever had.

The roads are really slippery, but I am not one bit worried, because my dad invents cool inventions. And he invented one called the Ice Be-Gone, on account of it melts ice on contact whenever you pull the cord that's attached to the bottle that's attached to our car.

So we are on our way to pick up my other friend, Gordy Rhinehart, when the car wheels start spinning on the ice.

"Let 'er rip, Angelwings," my dad says. Angelwings is one of the names he calls me sometimes.

I quickly yank on the cord, and the car

stops skidding, just like that!

"Ice Be-Gone does it again," says my dad, the coolest guy in the world.

Then we pull up in front of Gordy's house. He is standing there with Coach Rhinehart, his dad, waiting for us. Coach Rhinehart opens our car door. "Go get 'em, Gorderino!" he says, clapping Gordy on the back. This makes Gordy fall down, on account of Gordy is so very skinny and his dad is so very not.

But that's okay. Gordy just picks himself up and gets into our car, next to Gina Lash. "Don't break too many hearts," Gordy's dad says with a wink, and off we go.

"I brought you some Fishy Fish, Gina," says Gordy to Gina Lash, who he secretly loves. And he starts getting all wheezy like he always does when Gina's next to him.

Me and Gina and Johnny help ourselves because Fishy Fish candies are our favorites!

Except like now when they're hard as rocks on account of they got frozen when Gordy was waiting outside in the freezing cold. Everybody spits them out, even Gina Lash, who will normally eat just about anything.

When we pull up to the ice-skating pond we are so excited, we can hardly wait to put on our skates. But then something not so exciting happens. . . . You will see what I mean after I tell you who *else's* car is driving up to the rink . . . Mrs. Brinks!

"Mrs. Brinks!" I'm the one who says, "What's *she* doing here? This isn't our school!"

"You don't think . . . ," Gordy wheezes, "she's going to be . . . our ice-skating teacher, do you?"

"No way, it's Saturday. Teachers can't teach on Saturdays," says Gina. "It's against union regulations—unless she's a scab."

Like I told you, Mrs. Brinks is our most

unfavorite teacher. And I don't think you'll be surprised that we are surprised to see her at our ice-skating pond. And we aren't very happy about it, either. But then her husband, Mr. Brinks, whose name is Connie, gets out of their car. We hear her tell him, "Be sure you're waiting by the curb at exactly one-fifteen!"

"Yes, dear," says Mr. Brinks, his voice like a mouse.

The car door slams shut, and the car drives away, taking Mrs. Brinks away with it, which is lucky for us.

All of us say, "Phew. So it's *Mr.* Brinks who's gonna be our teacher!"

"That's right, kids," says my dad. "Guess it's good he's *dressed* . . . for the ice." And then he winks.

Mr. Brinks's eyeglasses sparkle in the sun. He wears strange-looking fuzzy red earmuffs and a long coat with furry stuff on the collar.

"I'm just glad he's wearing clothes at all," says Gina.

We all laugh at that one, even my dad. See, we all think Mr. and Mrs. Brinks are nudists who like to spend their weekends nude.

If this makes you think about the Brinkses ice-skating naked, then you're just like me. But I don't think about it for long. Yuck. Ugh. Gross.

CHAPTER TWO

So then we step out of the car and wave good-bye to my dad. Gordy Rhinehart takes off his coat. And he is wearing a shimmery, ruffly shirt, just like they wear on TV.

Johnny Abatti is dressed to play hockey, even though he doesn't know how to skate yet. Gina Lash looks puffier than she usually does in her puffy red parka. We put on our skates and step onto the ice *verrry* carefully.

Mr. Brinks is taking forever to take our

attendance. Meanwhile all of us can barely stand up. My ankles keep caving in. Gina keeps falling down on her behind.

Mr. Brinks has an official attendance list on his clipboard. "Okay, Angela is here, so I'll just put a little check in this box next to her name. And . . . Gina's here, check. And Gordy's also here, so that's another little check. . . ."

So far it is not so fun on account of it is not fun waiting for Mr. Brinks to finish, and not fun trying to stand up on my skates. I am so busy trying to keep my ankles from caving in that I almost miss what Mr. Brinks says next.

"Hmm, where's Nanette Manoir?"

This can't be, I think to myself—Nanette is going to ice-skate too? And then the next thing that happens is that I hear a voice. *Her* voice. Ninnie Poo's voice.

"Over here! I'm over here!"

Am I just imagining things? No such luck. I look over and see it, the Manoirs' gigantic black giant-sized Town Car.

Nanette stands there, in a stupid plaid coat, shaking her golden, baloney curls. Their gardener, Alfredo, is bending down to shovel a path through the snow for her. What is she doing at *our* ice-skating class, is what I want to know, and besides, I thought the cold isn't good for her sensitive, un-French skin!

"I'm simply waiting for Alfredo to clear a path for me," she calls to us. "It's so hard keeping gardeners busy in the winter, and I certainly don't want to get any snow on my new *après*-skate boots!"

Then Alfredo helps her step out of her *après*-skate boots for snot-noses and into her skates.

"Wow, Nanette," says Gordy Rhinehart,

staring at her boots, "Those boots are so next year."

"They're more than just next year, Gordy Rhinehart," says Nanette as she steps onto the ice. "They're pure, ermine-lined *après-skate boots!*"

She twirls around on the ice, and it is at this point that it comes into my mind that she is *not* a beginning skater. She swooshes to a show-off stop near where we are standing, or at least trying to stand, covering all of us with a layer of ice.

"Well done, Nanette!" says Mr. Brinks, clapping with his mittens. "Now let us begin. Please be very careful. We don't want any strains, sprains, or other nasty pains. Everyone follow me. Step, step, gliiiiiiide. Step, step, gliiiiiiide."

Me and Gordy and Johnny try to follow Mr. Brinks. Gina just falls on her butt.

Ninnie Poo flies past us. "Look at me! I can do it backwards!" she calls.

"Very nice, Nanette!" calls Mr. Brinks. "But remember: A slow skater is a safe skater!"

"I don't want to go slow," Bratette says as she skates circles around us.

"Whatever you say, Nanette," Mr. Brinks tells her.

Oh brother, I think.

"Hey!" yells Gina Lash. "Wasn't this supposed to be a beginners' class?" And then she falls down again.

"Yeah, Nanette!" I yell. "For someone who has never been in one before!"

"But you see," calls Ninnie Poo, "I've never been in a *public* skating class, Angela Anaconda. I've only had private lessons, *à la carte!*"

"Come along, everybody," Mr. Brinks is saying. "Heads up. Arms out. Step, step, gliiiiiiide."

"When are we gonna learn the slap shot?" asks Johnny Abatti.

Nanette just keeps showing off. She whooshes past Gina Lash and makes her fall onto her behind again.

"Step, step, gliiiiiiide," Mr. Brinks keeps saying over and over again.

And then, if you can believe it, Gordy Rhinehart all of a sudden looks like he knows how to do it. "Hey, look! I'm gliding! I'm *gliiiiiiiding,* everybody!" he calls, and his ruffles ruffle in the wind.

"Well, look at *me!*" cries Nanette as she zooms past. "I'm *really* skating!"

"Oh, my!" says Mr. Brinks. "Aren't you the bee's naked knees! Impressive, Nanette, very impressive! Look, Angela. Look, Gina. See how *she* does it?"

Yeah, sure, more like, I see how she ruins our class. So, just like usual, Nanette Manoir is the teacher's pet. "We'd better learn to skate soon, Gina Lash," I tell my friend. "My ankles are tired!"

"Your ankles and *my* butt," says Gina, falling down again.

Nanette swoops up to Johnny Abatti. "*Bonjour,* John. Care to skate with a *real* skater?"

She grabs him by the hand. Which is something she always tries to do. Except that this time she starts to spin him around and around, faster and faster. There is no way he can stop or do anything except yell, "WHOAAA!"

Mr. Brinks thinks it is great. "Magnificent! Wonderful!" he says. Then, all of a sudden, he must have stopped thinking it was so great. "Oh, *my!*"

Nanette has come to a sudden stop. "Ta-da!" she says.

But Johnny Abatti does not come to a sudden stop. When Nanette lets go of his hand, he goes flying. And when he goes flying, you won't believe where he goes flying to.

"John!" I hear Ninky-Slinky say. "'Ta-da' means 'the end'! Come back here this instant!"

But Johnny Abatti cannot come back. He is too busy flying across the ice, without being able to stop, straight at Gordy, who crashes into Gina, who crashes into me.

My life flashes before my eyes.

CHAPTER THREE

So, thanks to Ninnie Poo Manoir and her unbeginner ice-skating, my broken arm gets broken. And I have to listen to my dumb brothers say dumb things. My brother Derek says, "Geez, Angie-pants, didn't they teach you how to fall?"

"Yeah," says my brother Mark, "maybe you need lessons on how to take skating lessons."

See what I mean? But the good thing is that I got a Day-Glo cast, and all of my friends at school want to sign it.

The bad thing is that Candy May is the first one in my class to try to sign it, and she takes forever to sign her name. She's just gotten to the "a" in "Candy," when who should open her big un-French mouth but Nanette.

"Excuse me, Mrs. Brinks, but since it's taking Candy May such a long time to sign Angela Anaconda's cast, perhaps we need an example of proper signature form. And since I study calligraphy with the famous French calligrapher Pierre La Plume, I would be more than happy to volunteer."

And then Mrs. Brinks, who thinks that Nanette Manoir is some kind of a genius, says, "Why, thank you, Nanette dear. How very generous of you to share your refined skills with the class."

And the next thing I know, Nanette has

grabbed the pen out of Candy May's hand and is writing her name in huge big letters that take up my whole entire cast.

That night I sit on my bed and look down at my cast that she has wrecked. It doesn't do any good to turn the light off, because my Day-Glo cast glows in the dark so I can still see her name. I am stuck with it. Oh brother, I think, and then I turn the light on, then I turn it off, then on, then off.

And then in my mind I start thinking. Like I told you before, I do a lot of making things up in my head, which my dad says is fine to do. In my head I can imagine anything I want, even if it's about things I would like to do to a Certain Nasty Someone that she actually deserves but that I wouldn't actually be allowed to do in real life. I would only *imagine* doing them. So this is what I imagine doing:

Here comes Ninnie Poo, Star of the Nanette Scapades, me the Skating Announcer Angela Anaconda announces! Watch as she and Gliding Gordy glide through their routine. The naked judges, who all happen to look just like Mr. Brinks, say, don't you look divine, Ninkie-Wink. The bee's naked knees, Little Nin.

The crowd is cheering on account of your excellent performance, but too bad Gordy Rhinehart only knows one move. I like to glide, he will tell you, as he picks you up and twirls you around, then throws you flying through the air.

Whoops! Watch out, Little Nin, I say as you land on your behind. That ice sure is slippery. Perhaps my dad's Ice Be-Gone is just what you need. Here comes Angela Anaconda to the rescue, I will tell you while I spray the Ice Be-Gone all around you. Oops. So sorry, Little Nin, but it appears you have fallen right through the hole I have accidentally made in the ice.

"Save me! Save me!" you will tell me as you splash around in the icy water wearing nothing but your fancy pink skating outfit. "These waters are filled with millions of Fishy Fish who would like to chew on my sensitive skin!"

Bye-Bye, Nanook of the North, I will tell you as you float out to sea and the Land of the Midnight Sun, which is what I think they call Alaska. Here come the Eskimo babies, who learned to skate before they could even walk. Uh-oh! They have built an igloo out of you! Or should I say . . . UG-loo!

But here comes Angela, paddling up in my kayak. Never fear, my fake French friend, I will gladly come to your rescue, except—look! You are frozen just like a hockey puck! In fact, here comes Johnny Abatti, who really thinks you are a hockey puck, my prissy polar pal.

"Help me, help me, O Great One, Angela

Anaconda, whose skating ability would be far superior to mine if I, Nanette, hadn't so rudely interrupted your beginners' class and broken your arm," you will tell me.

But then when I come to rescue you, I can't help thinking, did somebody say, Na-NET?

Then, WHAM! Into the net Hockey Puck Nanette will go! Angela ONE, Nincompoop . . . NOTHING! The crowd goes wild and they all yell, "An-ge-la! An-ge-la! An-ge-la!"

"An-ge-la! ANGELA!"

Oops. I open my eyes and I am no longer imagining things. It is morning! My friends Gina, Gordy, and Johnny are standing outside my bedroom window, calling my name— "An-ge-la!" The sun is streaming in.

"Hey, Angela! We're going to shovel snow for the shut-ins!" calls Gina Lash. "Want to come?"

"You bet," I yell down to them.

CHAPTER FOUR

So there I am with my friends, blasting away the snow with my bottle of Ice-Be-Gone because, on account of my broken arm, I can't shovel like Gina, Johnny, and Gordy. Then all of a sudden we hear a rumble from across the street.

And going toward the Manoirs' driveway is Alfredo driving a tractor, and attached to the tractor is a fancy little sled and on the sled is none other than Nanette Manoir and her poofy French poodle Oo-la-la, getting a free ride as usual. The tractor stops right in front of us, spraying snow all over where we have just cleared it.

"Oh, I am ever so sorry," says Nanette, who does not sound one bit sorry at all. "I'd gladly offer to help if I weren't wearing my pure ermine-lined *après*-skate boots, which would be ruined if just a speck of snow were to touch them. So if you'll excuse me, I'll just go drink some *imported* hot chocolate in front of our *roaring* fireplace! *Bonne chance!*"

We watch them drive away, this time spraying even more snow where we have been clearing it. Across the street, which is where the Manoirs live, we watch Ninnie Poo step out of her boots and hand them to Alfredo. Then she goes inside.

Then we see Alfredo give us a look. He puts the boots down, right there on the driveway. And he looks at us again.

That is when we get an idea.

"Are you thinking what I'm thinking, Angela Anaconda?" says Gina Lash.

"If you're thinking what I'm thinking," I tell her.

And then three shovels full of snow belonging to Gina, Johnny, and Gordy just *happen* to land on those pure, ermine-lined *après*-skate boots by accident. Accidentally on purpose!

We all stare at the boots with the lumps of snow in them. And then we hear the tractor again. And along comes Alfredo on the tractor. He revs the engine and winks at us, and then does something we never expected him to do. He dumps a huge pile of snow on top of Nanette's fancy boots.

By the time we have already almost fallen down in the snow from laughing, I say,

"Good thing those boots are *so* next year, Gordy Rhinehart. Because I don't think Ninnie Poo's going to be seeing them until next spring!"

Story Number Two

Touched
by an
Angel-A

CHAPTER ONE

In case you think that I have never tried to be nice to Nanette Manoir, let me tell you that I *have* tried. But she is not easy to be nice to, on account of the fact that she is not nice.

Ask Josephine Praline, who is training to become a saint and who says she sees good in everybody—even Nanette. She will tell you about the time she tried to make me see some good in Nanette too.

It all began during nature science. Me and my friends and a certain person I just mentioned, who is mean and not nice to anyone, are studying about caves.

"So, remember, children," says my teacher, Mrs. Brinks, "stalactites hang tightly while stalagmites stand mightily!" She points to the picture of the cave. "Have you ever seen anything as impressive as those stalactites?"

Johnny Abatti, my dim-witted friend, points at the ceiling. "You mean more impressive than Uncle Nicky's Eternal Spitball?" he asks. Johnny's Uncle Nicky is famous. And Uncle Nicky's Eternal Spitball that has been hanging like a stalactite from the ceiling of our classroom since before I even was born is even more famous than Uncle Nicky himself.

We all look up and stare at it. Johnny Abatti turns around in his seat. "Uncle

Nicky used to eat paste, so it's never coming down," he tells us.

"I hope you're wrong as usual, John," says Nanette Manoir. "The sooner that hideous aberration of school property that you and a *certain* tasteless person whose initials are AA"—and she looks right at me—"call a 'spitball' comes down from that ceiling the better."

"You mean the sooner you're allergic to your own brain the better, Nanette Manure," I whisper to Johnny.

But Josephine Praline must have heard me. "Angela Anaconda," she says nervously in that quiet way of hers. "You must confess, that wasn't a very nice thing to say. If you harbor such feelings in your heart, you'll never be touched by an angel. And if you're never touched by an angel, your life will be nothing but trouble."

I roll my eyes. "Sure, Josephine Praline, whatever you say," I reply. Besides, who needs to be touched by an angel, anyway, I think to myself.

But then some strange things start to happen. Because the next thing I know—YUCK!—the Eternal Spitball that was supposed to be eternally attached to the ceiling falls right onto my desk! And not onto Johnny's desk or Gina's desk or anyone else's desk but onto *my* desk, mine!

"Hallelujah!" cries Josephine Praline. "It's a sign from Above!"

But Mrs. Brinks does not think that it is a sign from Above. She thinks it is a sign that I have done something I wasn't supposed to do. Which is not fair, because I haven't done any such thing. A giant shadow shaped like a refrigerator with a waistline falls over my desk. I look up to see Mrs. Brinks's angry face. "Dispose of your repugnant handiwork at once!" she yells at me.

"But I didn't do anything!" I protest. "It's Uncle Nicky's!"

"Don't be ridiculous," she tells me. On account of Uncle Nicky had dropped out of Tapwater Springs Elementary about twenty-five years ago, I get sent to clean the chalkboard erasers. When I stand up to go, Josephine Praline whispers to me, "That wouldn't have happened if you had been touched by an angel."

CHAPTER TWO

But I am still not so sure about needing an angel to touch me. Even though the next thing that happens to me should have been pretty convincing.

"The spitball was not a sign from Above," I have just finished saying to Gina Lash and Johnny Abatti as I brush the chalk dust off and walk onto the playground. "It was an accident!" And just when I say it, a kickball hits me from behind.

"That was just an accident too!" I say, picking myself up.

But accidents just keep happening to me all day for the rest of the day. Like getting knocked down at the swing. And then my lunch bag breaks, and my sandwich falls on the ground. And somebody steps right on it.

Then Gina Lash says—as if I didn't notice this myself—"Angela, there's a footprint on your sandwich!"

"Accidents happen," I reply—just before getting splashed by a mud puddle.

"What a recess!" I say to myself in the bathroom while I am washing off all of the mud. "If I didn't know better, I'd say I was jinxed!"

"You're not jinxed, Angela Anaconda," says a voice. "You just need an angel."

I look up on account of I think it may be a voice from Heaven. But no one is there. So

I look down. And I see someone's shoes in one of the stalls. "Josephine Praline?" I say. "Is that you?"

"Yes, my child, I am with you. And your guardian angel would be too, if you could learn to love your enemies."

"Sure, sure," I say, still not believing her . . . until the faucet breaks on the sink, which it has never done, and water sprays all over the place—and Mrs. Brinks walks in right when it happens.

"What in the name of Lady Godiva!" she exclaims, looking at all the water. "Angela Anaconda, I think you know what this means."

I guess you know what it means too. I have to go clap more of Mrs. Brinks's erasers, which I have already clapped a million times. But, anyway, I clap those erasers as hard as I can. And then there is a white cloud of white chalk dust and I might think I am seeing things, but I really do see Josephine Praline drift by like a ghost with a little, tiny teeny angel on her shoulder.

"Hey, Josephine!" I call. "Wait up!" On account of I am starting to think that maybe she is right after all. Maybe I really do need an angel.

CHAPTER THREE

So that is it. I finally decide that maybe I'd better try to act nice to everyone. Because I sure need a guardian angel, big-time. I stand up on the toilet seat so I can talk about this to Josephine, who is in the next stall.

"If you want to be touched by an angel, you have to learn to be kind and good. And you must learn to love your enemies."

"Okay." I shrug.

"*Even* your Nanettes," she says firmly.

"On second thought," I say, "maybe I could just get a rabbit's foot," and right then I fall into the toilet. Which means it is definitely time to act nice—even to Nanette.

In the cafeteria, I tell Gina Lash and Johnny Abatti that I plan to try to be nice to Nanette. They can hardly believe their own ears.

"You hafta do what?" asks Johnny Abatti.

"You heard me," I say. "I have to be nice to Ninnie Wart. Otherwise I'm doomed to a life of trouble my whole life."

And then I hear Ninnie Poo, who is sitting a few tables away, say, "Oh, poo! Cook forgot to remove the crusts on my cucumber sandwich again!"

This is my chance to try to be nice to my enemy. Only I can't just give her my stepped-on sandwich, on account of it was stepped on. So when Johnny Abatti is temporarily blinded by his lunch by getting

sauce in his eye, I grab his plate of spaghetti and bring it over to her table.

"Here you go, Nanette," I say as nice as I can be. "A crust-free lunch just for you."

"*Spaghetti?*" sneers Nanette. "The only pasta that touches *my* lips is angel hair."

I can't help it: This makes me so mad, I imagine pouring the spaghetti right over her perfect baloney curls. That would show her. But instead of that, what really happens is I slip, and Johnny's spaghetti flies out of my hands and lands on me without any curls. Have I tripped? Maybe. But then again . . . maybe not.

"She started it!" I say out loud so if there is an angel listening it can hear me.

Later that day Josephine Praline comes up with more advice. "Try offering her something she truly *needs,* Angela Anaconda."

Okay, fine, I am thinking, and it starts to rain. So I decide I will share my umbrella with her.

"Angela Anaconda, give me that! You almost put out one of my sparkling eyes!" is what she says. And she grabs *my* umbrella and walks all the way to her house with me running after her like all of a sudden it was her umbrella. She stays dry. I get wet. In my wetness I find it hard to think nice things to think about Nanette. But I tell myself I will keep trying.

The next morning I surprise her by waiting outside her house with another umbrella. Who cares if it isn't even raining anymore?

"Hi, Nanette!" I say as nice as possible. "I practiced all night and now I know how to hold an umbrella just like they do in France, where you are most certainly from."

I try to hold the umbrella for her so the sun's rays won't damage her sensitive skin. I shield her from the sun all the way to school, but when we get there, all she does is tell Mrs. Brinks that I was chasing her with my umbrella.

"I was only trying to act nice," I say.

Josephine Praline shakes her head. "Angela, Angela, it's not enough to *act* nice to Nanette. You have to *be* nice in your heart. Don't lose faith, my child," says Josephine. She tears a piece of paper out of her notebook. "Here. Make a list of all the things that are nice about Nanette. Just find one thing and an angel will find you."

What I'd like to know is: Is Josephine Praline praying for a miracle or something?

CHAPTER FOUR

So that's how I have ended up sitting in my room, trying to think of just one nice thing to write down about Nanette Manoir. "There is nothing nice about Nanette," I say, staring at the blank piece of paper in front of me. "Think, think, think," I tell myself.

And that's when it happens. I think I see the Angel Josephine and she is floating on a cloud right in front of me in my very own room.

"Take my hand, Angela Anaconda," says the

Angel Josephine. "Together we shall find the Nanette who has been forgotten. The nice Nanette."

So I take her hand, and we fly away out the window on a cloud and look for the nice Nanette.

The first place we come to is a sandbox. There we can see little baby Nanette and little baby Angela playing together.

"Observe," says Angel Josephine. "Innocence playing."

"Excusez-moi," we hear the little Nanette say to the little Angela. "I'm afraid this zone has been set aside for the construction of a new freeway for my Santa Barbara Susie's new convertible." And Alfredo her servant comes along and mooshes little Angela's sand castle, and makes her cry.

"Hmm," says the Angel Josephine, frowning. "Oh well, she's just . . . a baby!"

Next we see Nanette walk into a hospital room. She is dressed like a volunteer worker.

"Ah," says Angel Josephine. "Observe Nanette, merciful and caring."

"What beautiful flowers, Mrs. Moran," we hear Nanette say to the old woman lying in the bed. "But seeing as they spoil your view of the parking lot, I'm sure you'd like me to have them." And she takes them from the vase. And poor old Mrs. Moran can do nothing, only moan.

Then Angel Josephine starts looking a little like she doesn't like what she sees.

So next we fly to Nanette's bedroom. There she lies sleeping, wearing a fancy silk gown and matching eye covers.

"Ah," says Angel Josephine. "There's nice Nanette. Innocent in her dreams."

Nanette wakes up.

"Hello, Nanette," says Angel Josephine. "I am an angel."

"I really don't care if you're Mother Teresa," says Nanette. "How dare you ruin my beauty sleep! Now scoot, scoot, scoot!"

"But I'm here to show Angela . . . ," says Angel Josephine.

"ANGELA? That does it. I'm getting security."

As she pulls the alarm, we fly out the window. Angel Josephine turns to me, and she's not looking too happy. "You were right, Angela. There isn't anything nice about Nanette."

I sigh. "So now I guess I'll never be touched by an angel."

Angel Josephine shrugs. "It could be worse. You could be just like her!"

Just like her . . . just like her . . . just like . . . hey!

I open my eyes and Angel Josephine is gone and I am sitting in my room. But the good thing is I have finally thought of an idea for my list!

CHAPTER FIVE

The next morning when I get to school I can't wait to show Josephine my list. "I did it! I did it, Josephine! I actually found a lot of nice things to say about Nanette!"

"I knew you would, my child," says Josephine. She peers at my list and begins to read: "One, she's not a twin . . . two, she doesn't have a clone . . . three, there is only one of her."

Josephine looks up at me. "Well, that's

not quite what I had in mind, Angela, but . . . it'll do."

"Does that mean I'll be touched by an angel?" I ask her.

"Perhaps," says Josephine, and she makes that dreamy look where her eyes half disappear up into her head, "perhaps you already have been."

Is that a golden halo around Josephine? It sure looks like one to me. Or maybe it is just the school bell behind her head? I can't be sure.

The bell rings. I start to walk into the school, and a kickball comes flying straight at me.

But guess what?

It misses!